Sitting Down to Eat

Story by BILL HARLEY
Pictures by KITTY HARVILL

AUGUST HOUSE
LittleFolk

To Danny Block and Zachary Zerphy,
two boys who would open the door for any elephant
(with thanks to Martín Espada)
—B.H.

To Ted, for nudging me into a bright, bold, brave new world.
—K.H.

Text © 1996 by Bill Harley.
Illustrations © 1996 by Kitty Harvill.

Published 1996 by August House LittleFolk,
P.O. Box 3223, Little Rock, Arkansas 72203, 501-372-5450.

Book design by Harvill Ross Studios Ltd., Little Rock, Arkansas

Manufactured in Korea

10 9 8 7 6 5 4 3   PB

LIBRARY OF CONGRESS CATALOGING-IN-PUBLICATION DATA

Harley, Bill, 1954–
Sitting down to eat / Bill Harley ; illustrated by Kitty Harvill.
    p.   cm.
Summary: In this cumulative story, a young boy agrees to share his snack with
an ever-growing menagerie of animals, each insisting that there is room for one
more.
ISBN-13: 978-0-87483-460-4(hc)
ISBN-10: 0-87483-460-0(hc)
ISBN-13: 978-0-87483-603-5(pbk)
ISBN-10: 0-87483-603-4(pbk)
[1. Animals—Fiction. 2. Counting. 3. Stories in rhyme.]
I. Harvill, Kitty, 1958– , ill.   II. Title.
PZ8.3.3H2125Si   1996
[E]—dc20   95-53738

The paper used in this publication meets the minimum requirements
of the American National Standards for Information Sciences—
permanence of Paper for Printed Library Materials, ANSI.48-1984

I was sitting down to eat,
just about to begin,
when someone knocked on the door and said,
"Can I come in?"

When I opened up the door, what did I see?
It was a great big elephant looking at me!
I said, "Oh no! What can I do?"
"If you've got enough for **one**," she said,
        "you've got enough for **two**."

"I've got enough for me, yes, that's true.
If I've got enough for me,
        I've got enough for you.
        Come on in!"

"Thank you," said the elephant.

So we both sat down,
just about to begin.
Someone knocked and called,
"Can I come in?"

I opened up the door,
　　　　and what did I see?
It was a great big tiger growling at me.
I said, "Oh no! This can't be!"
"If you've got enough for **two**," he growled,
　　　　"you've got enough for **three**."

"I've got enough for elephant, yes, that's true.
If I've got enough for her,
　　　　I've got enough for you.
　　　　Come on in!"

"Thank you," growled the tiger.

So **three** sat down,
        just about to begin.
Someone knocked on the door and puffed,
        "Can I come in?"

When I opened up the door, what did I see?
It was a big brown bear, huffing at me.
I said, "Oh no! Not one more!"
"If you've got enough for **three**," she huffed,
"you've got enough for **four**."

"I've got enough for elephant
and tiger, that's true.
If I've got enough for them,
I've got enough for you.
Come on in!"

"Thank you," huffed the bear.

Now **four** sat down,
      just about to begin.
Someone knocked and snarled,
      "Can I come in?"

I opened up the door, and what did I see?
It was a great big lion roaring at me.
I said, "Oh no! Not more, please!"
"If you've got enough for **four**," he roared,
"then **five** can squeeze."

"I've got enough for elephant, tiger and bear,
yes, that's true.
If I've got enough for them,
I've got enough for you.
Come on in!"

"THANK YOU," roared the lion.

Now there were **five**,
    just about to begin.

Someone knocked on the door
and moaned, "Can I come in?"

When I opened up the door,
what did I see?
A very large hippo
blubbering at me.

I said, "Oh no! Now I'm in a fix!"
"If you've got enough for **five**," she blubbered,
  "you've got enough for **six**."

"I've got enough for elephant, tiger, bear
  and lion—yes, that's true.
If I've got enough for them,
  I've got enough for you.
  Come on in!"

"Thank you," blubbered the hippo.

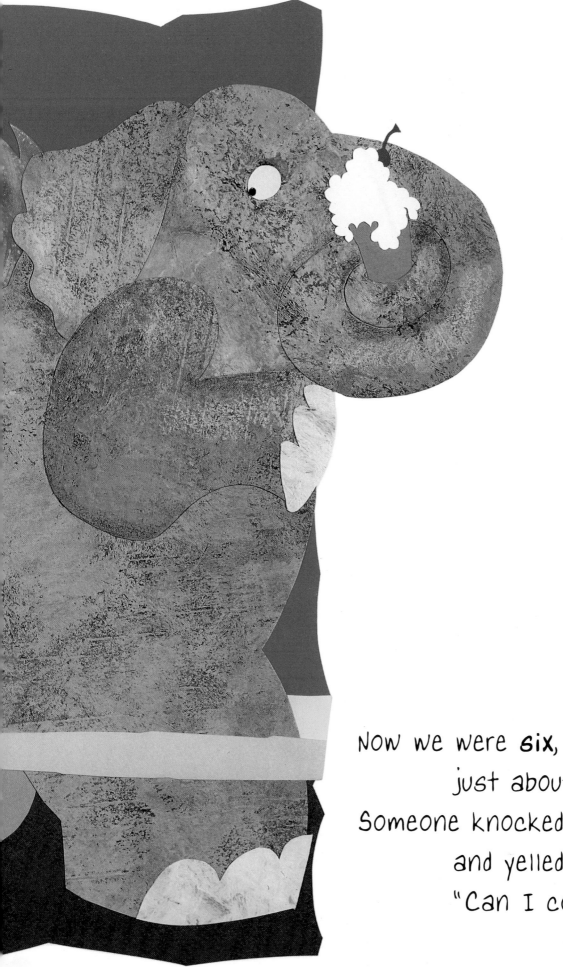

Now we were **six**,
          just about to begin.
Someone knocked
          and yelled,
          "Can I come in?"

I opened up the door,
    and what did I see?
A big rhinoceros
    snorting at me.
I said, "Oh no!
    Where will I sit?"
"If you've got enough
    for **six**," he snorted,
    "then **seven** will fit."

"I have enough for elephant,
    tiger and bear,
    lion and hippo,
    yes, that's true.
If I've got enough for them,
    I've got enough for you.
    Come on in!"

"Thank you,"
    snorted the rhinoceros.

There were **seven**
all sitting,
just about
to begin.
Someone knocked
on the door
and sang,
"Can I
come in?"

7

When I opened up the door, what did I see?
A big blue whale spouting water at me.
I said, "Oh no! You're much too late!"
"If you've got enough for **seven**," she spouted,
        "you've got enough for **eight**."

"I've got enough for elephant,
        tiger and bear,
        lion, hippo,
        and rhino, too.
If I've got enough for them,
        I've got enough for you.
        Come on in!"

"Thank you," spouted the whale.

8

It
was
crowded
with
eight,
just
about
to
begin.

Someone
knocked
and
cried,
"Can I
come
in?"

When I opened up the door, what did I see?
It was a bumpy crocodile smiling at me.
I said, "Oh no! Not you, too!"
"If you've got enough for **eight**," he smiled,
"then **nine** will do."

"I have enough for elephant,
      tiger and bear,
      lion and hippo,
      rhino and whale—
      yes, that's true.
If I've got enough for them,
      I've got enough for you.
      Come on in!"

"Thank you," smiled the crocodile.

There were **nine** squeezed in,
        just about to begin.
Someone tapped on the door and said,
        "Can I come in?"

When I opened up the door, what did I see?
It was a teeny tiny caterpillar
        looking at me.
I said, "Oh no! What can I do?
I don't think there's room for you."
She said,

        "Yes, there is.
        I'm sure there's room."

                She crawled in the door . . .

and the house went

ABOUT THE STORY

Song and story have always been next-door neighbors. As a singer and storyteller, I'm fascinated by the connection between the two and don't like to separate them. It seems only natural to me that "Sitting Down to Eat" started as a song and ended up a story in a picture book. While it has my name on it, the story is really based on stories and songs I've learned along the way.

I wrote the song "Sitting Down to Eat" as a "zipper" song with my son Noah. A zipper song is a song in which different words are substituted in each verse—in this case the animal that comes and visits and the noise that animal makes. "This Little Light of Mine" is a well-known example, in which the first line is changed, but the rest of the song remains the same. *This little light of mine* changes to *deep down in my heart* and then to *all over the world*. Lee Hays and Pete Seeger wrote "If I Had a Hammer," changing *a hammer* to *a bell* and *a song* in each succeeding verse. These songs are easy to sing and adaptable to many situations, since the words can change. Many song collections have numerous examples of zipper songs, which let children help create the song.

"Sitting Down to Eat" worked well as a zipper song. Noah and his friends liked it since they got to suggest ridiculous animals (it quickly went from *rhinoceros* to *tyrannosaurus rex* to *giant pigs*). The more animals that came into the house, the funnier it got. The problem then became what to do with all the animals.

That's when the song became a story. I immediately thought of all the cumulative stories there are in folk literature. From "The House that Jack Built" to "The Gingerbread Man" to "Chicken Little," storytellers have always liked to add one character or situation on to another, much like a zipper song. The solution to my story presented itself in the form of "The Mitten," an eastern European tale about a child who loses his mitten in the forest. There are several versions of the story in print, the most popular being Jan Brett's. One by one, the animals climb in the mitten to stay warm, until the smallest of them all, the mouse, creeps in and the mitten explodes. What a perfect solution! It is both ridiculous and logical. I borrowed it for the ending to my story, though the mitten is a house and the mouse is a caterpillar.

How to read the story? It sounds best out loud. It's a challenge to find a different voice for every different animal, but it certainly adds to the story. As you read the story, you will find the natural rhythms in the verse so that you, as a reader, can hesitate at the right moments, and the enthusiastic listener can fill in the space. And encourage your listeners to say "BOOM" together at the end!

—B.H.